A CHRISTMAS CARD *for* MR. McFIZZ

Story by Obren Bokich   *Pictures by Dan Lane*

THE GREEN TIGER PRESS
San Diego
1987

Color separations by Colorcraft, Hong Kong
The typeface is Stempel Schneidler set by TypeLink of San Diego
Printed and bound in Hong Kong
Manufactured in Hong Kong

For Carol Cummins and Dorothy and Del Lane

Mr. McFizz and Mr. Griswold were neighbors. Not neighbors in the sense that they had ever behaved in a neighborly fashion toward one another, but because they lived near each other.

Mr. McFizz lived in a burrow. Not one of those tacky, prefab burrows so quickly thrown together nowadays. His was of the solid old style, as he would have proudly told a visitor on a tour of his home, if he had ever had a visitor. Built beneath a centuries old oak tree, it was as sound and safe as could be, and it gave him great peace of mind.

When Mr. McFizz had first seen the burrow, it was what one might call a fixer-upper. The previous owner, the last of a long line of interesting creatures to live there, had left it a terrible mess. But Mr. McFizz could see what it might be with a little hard work and ingenuity.

Fortunately, there was nothing he enjoyed more than cleaning, so the job was a happy one. He didn't even mind when he had to pound a loose wall with his head till it was safe and firm. Soon, the burrow was better than new.

Mr. McFizz was so pleased with his handiwork, he made up a special housewarming song:

I've swept and scrubbed,
Repaired and replumbed,
Pounded and painted
And now I'm all done.

He took immense pride in his little home, so imagine his horror when a pack-rat family moved into the old hollow stump next door.

Mr. Griswold wasn't really a bad sort, just a little messy. A serious collector, he was forever finding treasures in other people's trash; treasures cheerfully dragged home and stockpiled against the day when they would come in handy.

Mr. McFizz could barely stand to look at the growing pile of rubbish in his neighbor's yard.

Sometimes it was left at his very door!

Finally, after much soul-searching and general trepidation, Mr. McFizz marched through the clutter to his neighbor's door.

It had taken him days to work up the courage to speak to Mr. Griswold about the terrible state of his house and yard, but Mr. McFizz never got to deliver his well-rehearsed speech on community standards, for no one answered his firm knock.

He was certain that he could feel the Griswolds' beady little eyes watching him, as he stomped back to his house in a huff.

The situation went from bad to worse. McFizz's irritation turned to disgust and disgust to loathing as the pile of refuse grew. With dull fascination, he watched as his neighbor's yard became a junk heap.

But it wasn't until December that his feelings about Mr. Griswold crystallized into a genuine hatred.

Like most fussy creatures, Mr. McFizz had few friends. In fact, if the absolute truth were known, he had none. Throughout most of the year, this didn't bother him, since he was generally occupied with his cleaning, but at Christmastime, he had to admit to a twinge of melancholy.

It was at Christmastime, while he was sorting through the bills and the letters addressed to "OCCUPANT," that he wished someone would send him even one little Christmas card.

Sometimes there would be nothing at all in his mailbox, not even a catalogue from a seed company.

He had always been able to deal with this situation. After all, one can't expect every-thing out of life. But one horrible day in December, after another fruitless trip to his mailbox, he noticed several large, square envelopes in Mr. Griswold's mailbox. Could it be?

Carefully he lifted the top envelope. It was neatly hand lettered. It said:

Mr. & Mrs. Griswold
(& little Griswolds)
3 Acorn Way
Forestville

He examined the other envelopes. They were all addressed to the Griswolds, and he was certain they were all Christmas cards.

Then he realized that Mrs. Griswold was standing on her porch, watching him.

How embarrassing!

Smiling weakly, and with studied casualness, he walked back to his house, the very picture of guilt.

This, however, was only one of many bad days for Mr. McFizz as he observed a steady flow of Christmas cards to the Griswold household.

One day there were so many cards Mr. Turner, the postman, couldn't fit them all into their mailbox and hand delivered the overflow right to their door.

Mr. McFizz was never so relieved to see a holiday pass as that Christmas. But instead of forgetting the whole unhappy affair, he worried about it well into the new year.

As Christmas approached again, a plot hatched in his troubled brain, which, I must say, was totally unworthy of this otherwise fine fellow.

Mr. McFizz's plan was a simple one. In late November, he bought every Christmas card that his limited savings would allow, and addressed them to himself. He mailed a few each day, increasing the volume as Christmas loomed nearer.

Then, knowing where Mr. Turner stopped for coffee each morning, he crept up on the unwary postman and actually stole the Griswolds' Christmas cards from his mail-pouch before he could deliver them!

I think it is safe to say that Mr. McFizz had gone completely off the deep end.

He then settled into what he thought would be a delightful daily routine of collecting his Christmas cards, watching the disappointed Griswolds, and addressing a few more to himself for the next day's delivery.

He thought this would be great fun, but an odd thing occurred. He found that he felt uncomfortable instead of victorious each day when he collected his armload of phony Christmas cards while Griswold's mailbox was bare.

One day, very close to Christmas, Mr. McFizz watched Mr. Griswold forlornly examine his empty mailbox, then walk sadly back to his little house. It was then that an even odder thing occurred. He found himself addressing a Christmas card, not to himself, but to Mr. Griswold.

A few days later, when he watched Mr. Griswold find his Christmas card in his mailbox, Mr. McFizz caught a glimmer of what Christmas is really all about. He felt warm and good inside.

But the best part was yet to come, for the very next day, he found a Christmas card in his mailbox that he had not addressed.

Not only did it wish him a Very Merry Christmas, but also a Happy New Year and, what's more . . .

it invited him to Christmas dinner at the Griswolds', where he met Mrs. Griswold and Mr. Griswold and numerous Griswold children . . .

and drank eggnog and sang Christmas carols before a roaring fire . . .

and tried desperately to work up the nerve to say something to his neighbor about cleaning up his yard.